DANGER GUYS

Blast Off

DANGER GUYS
Blast Off

by Tony Abbott

illustrated by Joanne Scribner

HarperTrophy
A Division of HarperCollinsPublishers

Library of Congress Cataloging-in-Publication Data
Abbott, Tony.
    Danger Guys blast off / by Tony Abbott ; illustrated by Joanne Scribner.
        p.   cm.
    Summary: Having discovered that the mad scientist Morbius has sabo-
taged the rocket ride at the Mayville carnival, Noodle and Zeek confront
him and his dangerous robot in an underground laboratory.
    ISBN 0-06-440520-6 (pbk.)
    [1. Science fiction.]   I. Scribner, Joanne, ill.   II. Title.
PZ7.A1587Dap   1994   93-31806
[Fic]—dc20   CIP
                                                                      AC

Typography by Stefanie Rosenfeld
1   2   3   4   5   6   7   8   9   10
❖
First Harper Trophy Edition

With love for Jane,
who started all this kid stuff

Blast Off

ONE

Ping!

That's how it all started.

My best friend, Zeek, and I were in my backyard. We were building rockets out of plastic soda bottles. That was my idea.

Then we were going to shoot them off with air from my bike pump. That was my idea, too.

I'm always thinking up things to do. Zeek says my brain is on overdrive. That's why he calls me Noodle.

Zeek is incredible. He loves adventure just like I do. And he's also the best all-around sports star in my class.

With my brains and his muscle, we

make a great team. We do everything together.

Anyway, there we were. I was just going to customize my rocket with some junk I had collected—a mirror, a hand buzzer, a paper clip, and a fat rubber band.

Then Zeek jumped up. "Noodle, do you hear that?"

"Hear what?"

"It sounded like, I don't know, ping!"

I listened. "Yeah," I said. "Ping. It's pretty far away."

"But, Noodle, I know that sound. It's the sound you make when you hit that thing with a huge hammer and the thing goes up and hits the bell and you win something." Zeek looked at me as if I should understand. "You know."

It took me a minute. "Do you mean like a Test-Your-Strength game at a carnival?"

Then it hit me. We stared at each other. We both jumped up.

"The Mayville carnival! Now till Tuesday! Rides! ROCKET RIDES!"

2

In a flash we were at the Mayville carnival. It had just opened for the day. Strings of white lights surrounded the park. Hundreds of people were there already.

In one corner a rock band on a wooden stage was playing loud music. In another corner were all the pizza and hamburger booths.

In the middle were dozens of rides swooping up and around like crazy. Whip-Dip, Sling Shot, Free-Fall. Kids were screaming their lungs out. Moms and dads were in shock.

"Excellent," I said. Then I spotted the Belgian waffle booth. "Whoa, Zeekie. First we eat, then we ride."

But Zeek was already gone. I didn't see him anywhere. I was about to call out for him when I heard that sound again.

Ping!

No way, I thought. Zeek is a whiz at sports, but even high school kids can't hit that bell.

Then I heard it again. *Ping!*

I whirled around. There was Zeek, running back from the Test-Your-Strength game. He was smiling and holding up his prize.

"Noodle, look. A Fizz Blaster 2000!"

It was pretty neat, all right. A super-long-range, heavy-duty squirt gun with a sleek green barrel and two monster water tanks on the sides.

"Cool, " I said.

"Yeah," he said. "I love these things. I'm sure it will come in handy." He looked at me and grinned. *"If you know what I mean."*

I grinned back at him. Sure I knew what he meant. Ever since our adventure with underground treasure thieves, we've been known officially as the Danger Guys, two buddies who get into pretty amazing adventures. There's nothing we can't handle. And we can always use great equipment.

Zeek slung the Blaster over his shoulder, nudged me, and pointed. I turned to look.

Incredible!

It was like a scene from an old space movie. A whole battalion of rockets was coming in slowly for a landing.

First came a bright red one with lightning streaks painted on the sides. Next to it was a green capsule with yellow lights blinking from front to back.

But best of all was a sleek purple triangle with green fins and a silver nose. It looked superfast, just rocking there, empty and waiting for us to get in.

"The waffles can wait," I said. "That rocket's got our name on it."

But before we could move, a funny guy in a long white coat and wild hair rushed up the stairs and plunked himself down in the purple rocket.

"It's mine," he said to us, with a weird smile. Then he wrinkled his nose and shut his eyes. And sneezed. *"Aaa-choo!"*

The attendant came right over and said, "Sorry, mister, only kids can go on this ride."

The guy in the white coat didn't like that. He started sneezing again. But finally he got out. "Have a rotten ride, boys," he said as he passed us. Then he sneezed again. About eight times!

"Wow," I said. "Strange guy. He looks familiar, though, doesn't he?"

Before I knew it, Zeek had strapped me in next to him in the purple rocket. Then we started our trip to the top of the ride.

"Now, Zeek," I said. "Don't get me wrong. I love rocket rides. Only I don't want to hear any funny noises, okay? My dad says you can always tell when something's going to go wrong with the car just by listening for the funny noises."

Rrrrrrrr!

"Like that. What was that?"

Rrrrrrrr. Ping, ping, ping!

"No problem, Nood. Somebody else must have hit the bell."

"Uh . . . I don't think so, Zeek. That was us."

All of a sudden the rocket began to jiggle. The back end wagged back and forth. The nose twisted up and down.

"Hey," I yelled. "None of the other rockets are doing this."

Then—*CRACK! CLUNK! PING!*—the rocket jerked completely around and bounced up.

That's when everything went blurry.

And the rocket broke loose.

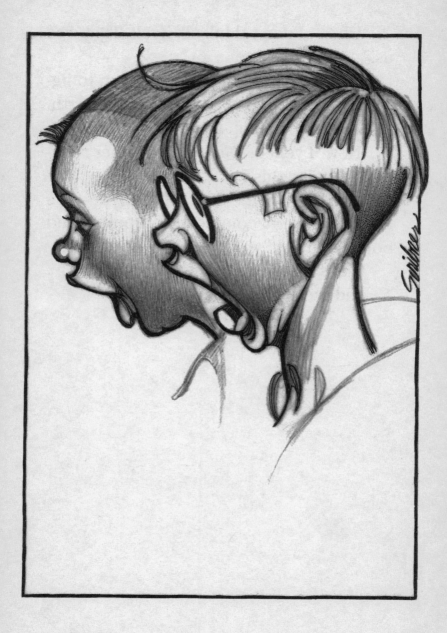

TWO

I looked at Zeek. He looked at me. Our mouths were open, but nothing came out.

Then—*vooom!*—our rocket plunged straight for the ground.

That's when our mouths started working.

"HELLLP!"

"Get us out of here!"

We zoomed straight at the rock band. Everyone screamed and scattered.

"Hey!" I cried. "Everybody's running away."

"No kidding, Noodle. They don't want to be under us when we crash!"

The ground rushed up at us. So this

was it. The end of the Danger Guys. I gave Zeek my last thumbs-up. He gave me one, too.

But just as we were about to blast into the drum set, the nose of the rocket tipped up. We went flying out through the cymbals and made a quick bounce over the bandshell.

"Whoa! Are we dead yet?" Zeek yelled.

"Not yet," I gasped. "But stay tuned!" We shot under the big food tent where hundreds of people were sitting munching away. They saw us and started to run.

"Noodle," Zeek yelled out. "Can't you control this thing?"

I jammed down all the switches on the control panel. I pulled the big stick in front of me.

"What are you doing that for? That stuff doesn't work!"

"I know that. But what do you want me to do, stick my arms out and grab something?" I gave him a look.

The rocket did a fast loop, bounced off

a picnic table, and shot toward the hamburger grill. A guy was flipping burgers high and letting them land on the hot grill. I could see the flames rising up.

"Shift your weight! We've got to veer out of the way!"

We leaned to one side, but I guess we leaned too far. We did a quick half-twirl. Instantly we were flying upside down through a stack of hot dog buns. I caught one and took a bite.

"Hungry?" I said, as we roared out of the tent. But Zeek wasn't laughing. He was down under the control panel.

I looked up. Straight ahead were the spokes of the giant Ferris wheel. They were turning fast.

"Zeek, we'll be sliced to ribbons!"

Vooom! The rocket made a sharp turn to the left and looped around the wheel.

"Whoa, Zeek! That wasn't luck. Something must be controlling this thing!"

Then Zeek sat up with a little black box in his hand. "Noodle, look. A radio."

I looked at it. "Yeah, but it's not the kind you talk into. Zeek, that's a radio-controller box."

"You mean . . ."

"Yep, this rocket is being radio controlled. Someone is—" That was all I could say.

The rocket suddenly jerked up over a bunch of kids buying cotton candy, leaped the fence around the carnival, and took off high over Mayville.

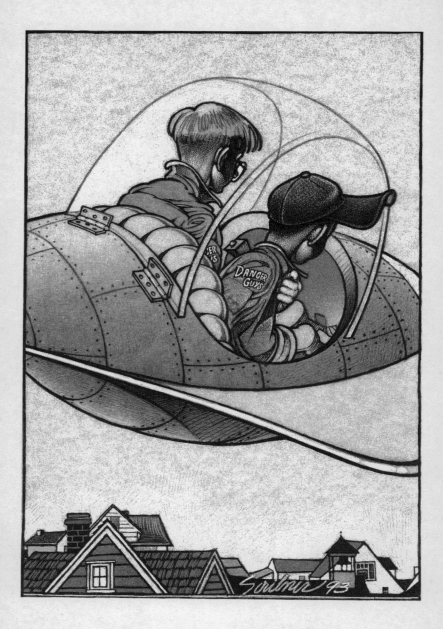

THREE

We cartwheeled over the library. Then we corkscrewed around the town hall dome about ten times. Finally we were jerked backward in our seats and we sailed up over Main Street.

Zeek wasn't happy. He looked sick. "Yeah, Noodle, I know. Cool ride. Good view. Great adventure. Terrific. But something basic here. *Just how are we going to get down?*"

Good question. We didn't have to wait long for the answer. A couple of seconds later the rocket swooped low and circled over a big brick building.

"Hey, Mayville School," I said. "We're

being pulled down to it. We're going to land."

Suddenly, the silver nose of the rocket dipped. Zeek grabbed my arm. "We're going to crash, you mean!"

We dropped straight down. The rocket hit the ground and skidded across the school parking lot toward the playground wall. Sparks sprayed up into our faces.

"We're not going to make it!"

Zeek was right. The rocket hit the wall fast and flipped over about a dozen times. On the third flip Zeek went flying into the jungle gym.

I hung on for another five flips and then took off screaming into the tire swing.

The rocket jolted up one last time and bounced over the mound at the edge of the playground. It stopped dead on the other side.

Then everything was quiet. Well, almost everything.

"Ohhh!" Someone was moaning. I looked at Zeek. I thought, How does he make that sound with his mouth closed? But when he started to talk I knew it wasn't him.

"Ohhh!"

Yeah, it was me. I was getting dizzy spinning on that tire. I was going to be sick. But Zeek ran over and pulled me off.

"I feel like human mush!" I said.

"We'd feel worse if we weren't wearing our Danger Guy jackets," Zeek said.

It was true. In these jackets you feel just about indestructible. Especially since our moms had put official Danger Guy patches on the shoulders.

Zeek grabbed his Fizz Blaster 2000 and stumbled over to the water fountain to fill it.

But when we looked out over the ridge at where the rocket had stopped, there was—nothing! No rocket! Nowhere!

"Wait a minute," I said. "There *was* a rocket here just a few minutes ago. The question is, Where did it go?"

Zeek knelt down and looked closely at

the grass. "Noodle, look at these lines in the ground."

We picked up sticks and started scraping. Soon we had scraped out a big square area, about the size of a garage door.

"What do you think it is, Nood?"

Before I could answer, the big square patch of ground started to move.

"Stand back!" I yelled. We both watched as the ground slid open in front of us. Then it stopped opening.

"It's a hatch," I whispered. "And there's a ladder down the side. Let's go in."

Zeek held my arm. I could tell he didn't like the idea.

"Noodle, I don't like the idea. A secret room hidden under the ground? No way. We have to call the principal, or maybe the police."

"Sure," I said. "Later. But that rocket is down there. And somebody just took us on a pretty wild ride. We've got to find out what it's all about."

I dangled my foot into the darkness and

felt for the first rung of the ladder. "Besides, we're a team, remember?" I gave him the thumbs-up.

Zeek broke into a smile. He gave me one, too. Then he tightened the strap on the Fizz Blaster 2000, zipped up his jacket, and put his foot on the ladder. "Okay, buddy, lead on."

Down we went. The ladder must have gone about twenty feet deep. The smell was creepy, like a doctor's office.

Finally I could see the floor just below me.

"Bingo," I whispered. "Wherever it is, we're here."

I was being so quiet.

I was going so slowly.

Then I set my foot down on the floor. And the whole world exploded.

FOUR

*Z*AAAP!

A sharp blast of blue light shot across the room, nearly piercing my ear.

Wham! The hatch slammed shut.

Fwiiing! Another blue beam shot out from the other side of the room.

Then another. And another.

"Crossfire!" Zeek yelped.

"*Laser* crossfire!" I cried. "Dive, or we're french fries!"

We both dived together. We slid down on our backs under the crossfire. Blasts of blue light hissed and spat deadly rays all around us.

Zaaap! Jing! Ssst!

"Now what, Noodle?"

I looked all around. We couldn't move. "Sorry, Zeekie. I've got only one idea and it's a bad one. I thought it over and it won't work. No way. I've got to think of something else."

Fwing! A beam blasted the floor near Zeek's head.

"What?" cried Zeek. "What wouldn't work? Maybe it would work. Maybe it would!"

Zzziiing!

I squeezed my hand into my jacket pocket and felt around. Got it! I pulled out the mirror I had stuffed in there that morning.

"Okay." I said. "The idea is to slip this mirror into the crossfire without zapping myself. Then it might send one of those death beams bouncing back to where it came from. You know, light bounces."

"Yeah, I remember," Zeek gasped. "Just like Mr. Vazny showed us in science class. That was cool!"

"Right. If it works. And if I don't turn myself into a fish stick."

"Just do it, Noodle. Or get the ketchup for both of us. I think I smell my sneakers burning!"

"Okay, here goes." Carefully I raised the mirror up into the crossfire.

One inch the wrong way and I was finished. Closer . . . Closer . . .

Zzzooop! A deadly blue beam slammed into the mirror and was zapped back right to where it came from.

KA-POW! Sparks burst out like fireworks from both walls. The whole room popped like a flash bulb on a camera. Suddenly, the laser beams fizzled and went dead.

I looked over at Zeek. He looked over at me.

"Yes!" he cried, punching the air with

his fist. "Noodle, you're a genius. You did it, smart guy!"

I smiled. "Yeah, sometimes it helps to have an idea or two. And a pocketful of junk."

"Right," said Zeek. "But now playtime is over. When you were doing your mirror trick, I saw a door. It's over this way."

Of course the door was locked.

Zeek started kicking and pounding on it.

Then I noticed something.

"Wait a second, pal. Maybe we're going about this the wrong way. You see this buzzer here? Maybe if we ring it the door will open."

Zeek shook his head. "Oh, sure. And maybe it'll open right into my kitchen and my mom will be waiting with lunch for us." He shook his head again. "No way."

"Yeah, I guess you're right." But I hit the buzzer anyway and the door jerked open. We tumbled through.

But it wasn't Zeek's kitchen. It was a long room. And instead of a floor there were stairs.

So we didn't walk right out like Zeek said we would. We crashed down the stairs over each other and landed in a heap.

At the bottom we sat up. We were sitting on a couch. A soft couch. With soft armrests and cushions.

"All right!" I said to Zeek. "This is okay, no?"

I started to give him a high-five when—

Clamp! Instantly a wide metal strap swung around from the side of the couch and pinned down my arm.

"Hey!"

Clamp! My other arm was trapped.

I looked over at Zeek. *Clamp! Clamp!* He was strapped down, too.

"Not okay, Noodle. Huh-uh. Not okay at all."

Suddenly, a sound crackled from all

around us. It sounded like a school announcement system being turned on. It was going to be loud.

Then a voice boomed in our ears.

"Welcome!" it said. "Welcome to my . . . *Aaa-CHOO!*"

FIVE

The sneezer!" I cried. "I can't believe it. The guy from the carnival! The guy with the white coat! The guy who—"

"I know, I know," said Zeek. "The guy who—"

"*Aaa-choo. AAA-choo. AAA-CHOO!*"

Each sneeze boomed over the announcement system like a nuclear explosion.

"Yuck!" cried Zeek. He closed his eyes and turned his face away from the noise.

Then the man in the white coat stepped out from the shadows at the far end of the room. Yeah, it was him. The same crazy hair. The same wild look on his face.

"Welcome, Mr. Newton and Mr. Pilinsky."

"Noodle, this is weird," Zeek whispered. "How does he know our names?"

"I'm trying to figure that out," I muttered under my breath.

I looked at the man. He was strange, all right. But something about him was very familiar. "Zeek, I know that face. I mean, even before the carnival. Doesn't he look like someone we know? I'm sure I know him, but—"

"STOP WHISPERING!" the man shouted. "I won't have whispering in my cla—I mean, in my laboratory!"

"Mr. Vazny!" I shouted. "Zeek! That's it! It's Mr. Vazny, our science teacher! It's him. I know it! It's—"

"SILENCE!" yelled the man in white. Then he stopped. His expression turned from a snarl to a smile. A weird smile.

"Call me . . . Morbius," he said quietly.

"But . . . you're . . . I mean . . . you're Mr. Vazny, our science teacher, aren't you? Sir? We haven't seen you around lately. Sir."

His eyes flashed another angry look.

Then he smiled again. "I . . . used to be Mr. Vazny. Now I am Dr. Morbius. Scientist!" He raised his hand and spoke over his shoulder. "Lights, please, Primus."

Something moved in the back of the room, and the lights slowly went up.

"Incredible!" I gasped.

It was a room just like the science lab at school, only bigger. There were smoking test tubes and beakers crowded on long tables. Maps of the stars were pinned to the walls. And a huge computer with a blinking screen whirred against the back wall.

"What is all this?" I asked.

"Behold! My secret underground command center."

Zeek glanced over at me as if he couldn't believe any of it. "His *what*?" he whispered.

"I built it myself," the man continued. "I took things from the school—a test tube here, a radio there. That is, until they found things missing and made me leave. The fools!"

31

Zeek couldn't take it anymore. "What is going on here?" he blurted out. "You mean you built this place *under the school*? Are you serious?"

"I AM A GENIUS!" Morbius screamed. "And now, with the rocket ride you brought me, I'll prove it to everyone!"

"Oh, yeah, what are you going to do, fly it into outer space?" Zeek started to laugh.

"Exactly!"

Zeek stopped halfway through his laugh. His mouth dropped open. Mine did, too.

"With the help of my X-5 Morbius Booster engine, I will explore space as no one has before. And after that . . ." He started to snort and chuckle so hard that his glasses slid down his nose. "After that I'll fly back and drop the Morbius Monster Bombs."

"Drop bombs?" I looked at Zeek. "Drop bombs on what?"

"Oh! That would spoil the surprise!"

Then Morbius started to laugh a really scary laugh, like somebody in a bad Halloween movie.

"Pssst, Noodle," Zeek whispered. "I must have missed something. Does he really mean it?"

"Oh, I mean it!" Morbius cut in. "And you little brats won't—won't—*aaa-choo!*—stop me either! Primus will make sure of that. Now, if you'll excuse me, I have a rocket to work on."

Morbius started laughing again and zapped a remote-control device at a door. It opened and he went through, cackling to himself and pushing his glasses up on his nose.

When he was gone, I told Zeek, "Listen, buddy, we've got to stop that nutty professor. Now!"

"Yeah, but what about this Primus guy he's talking about? What kind of name is *Primus*?"

I had a hunch what kind of name it was. But first things first. "Zeek, I'm squeezed tight in these straps. Are yours any looser?"

He squirmed around. "No way, these are solid. But wait a second. I think maybe . . ."

Zeek started to twist himself up. He almost disappeared into the couch cushions.

"What are you doing?" I asked. Zeek said something, but I couldn't make out what it was. His mouth was somewhere way under the rest of him.

A couple of seconds later he bounced up off the couch and stood on the floor in front of me, smiling. "Ta-da!"

"Cool! How did you do that?"

"Gymnastics, buddy. I do it all the time."

I could hear the sounds of Morbius working on the rocket. Drilling, hammering, whirring. And every now and then a crazy laugh.

"Hurry, Zeek. Monster Bombs, remember!"

"Right," Zeek said. Then he grabbed the

metal straps holding me down and started to breathe heavily. He gritted his teeth. He groaned. And he pulled.

"Work those muscles, Zeekie."

He pulled until his face began to turn purple.

Snap! One strap broke. Snap! The other strap broke.

"Just call me Schwarzenegger!" Zeek laughed. "Come on, pal. Next stop, Brainiac the Maniac."

But I couldn't budge. I saw something across the room.

"Um . . . Zeekie? What about *him*?"

"Him who?"

I took Zeek by the shoulders and turned him around.

"Oh. You mean *him*!" Zeek muttered. "Now I know what kind of name *Primus* is."

SIX

There, standing about ten feet away, was an enormous metal man. Tiny lights flashed around his huge head. And his *three* massive iron arms had ugly clamps at the ends.

Kkk-thunk! Kkk-thunk! The robot's heavy iron feet scraped across the floor.

"Oh, man! This isn't happening," Zeek moaned. "Tell me he's not real."

"Oh, he's real," I said. "He's just not human."

I took a quick look through the door. It was still open. "Listen, the rocket is down there. So is Morbius. We've got to stop him before it's too late."

"Sure," Zeek said. "But . . . you know. I mean, well, Iron Man. He's in the way."

"Maybe we can slip by him and get through the door," I whispered. "He seems pretty slow."

But in a blinding flash the robot reached for the remote and zapped it. The door slid shut.

"Oh-oh," I said. "Excellent aural receptors."

"Good ears, too."

"Okay, so maybe he's quick," I said. "But he's no match for the Danger Guys. And besides, we're talking about bombs here! So first we take out Robby the garbage can. Then we neutralize Dr. Destructo!"

Zeek grinned that old grin and jabbed his thumb in the air. I love it when he does that. It means we're in business.

But it wasn't so easy. Between us and all that stuff I said was the huge silver guy. He was coming at us. And he didn't look happy.

"I'll get the remote," Zeek shouted. He

lowered his Fizz Blaster 2000 straight at the remote. It was still in one of Primus's clamp-hands.

Fizz fizz fizz! A spray of water jetted through the air like an arrow. Direct hit! The remote flew out of the clamp-hand and hit the floor.

The robot didn't like that. He also didn't like it when I dived for it right under his big arms. I caught the remote and tossed it back behind me to Zeek.

"Noodle! Watch out!"

I tried to roll out of the way. Too late.

Primus grabbed me by the leg and threw me up in the air. Then he grabbed Zeek and threw him up. Then he started to, well, juggle us!

"Whoa-ooaa-ooaa! Let us down, you big . . ."

Yeah, he had good ears. *Wham!* I landed in a heap on top of the big computer. Zeek ended up by the couch. Luckily he still had his Blaster.

He pumped it and then aimed.

"Go for the eyeballs!" I called out. Zeek gave it all he had. But the spray just made Primus madder. He turned on Zeek with a vengeance.

Kkk-thunk! Kkk-thunk!

I had to do something. I jammed my hand into my pocket and fished around for something. What I came up with wasn't promising. A hand buzzer and a rubber band.

Great, if I wanted to make the tin man laugh, or if the rubber band could pierce metal.

"Noodle, it's too late for me. Run for your life!" yelled Zeek.

No way was I leaving my pal. Primus was lifting a metal desk high over his head and was about to crush Zeek with it.

There was no time to think. I wound the hand buzzer up all the way and wrapped the rubber band around the button. Then I threw it on the floor right in front of the robot.

Zzzzzzzzz!

Suddenly Primus stopped. He bent over slowly to look at the buzzer.

That was my chance. "Zeek! Move it!" I leaped off the computer right onto the iron guy's back.

That made Primus really mad. He started swinging me around.

"Whoa! You big—"

My legs crashed into the lab table. Test tubes and other junk went flying.

"Hold on, Noodle!" Zeek ducked out of the way and darted behind the robot. He slammed Primus behind the knees and the robot sank to the floor.

"All right, that trick still works!"

But the big guy wasn't finished yet. He growled a horrible growl, pulled himself back up, and swung me again.

Then Zeek yelled, "Noodle! His control panel. It's under his middle arm. I'll keep him busy while you go crazy with the switches."

Then Zeek did something really off the wall.

He started to sing.

"My mom taught me this one," he said.

He sang "Twinkle, Twinkle, Little Star."

It was horrible. Zeek can't sing at all.

The robot threw two of his arms up and covered what I guess were his ears. With the other one he tried to stop Zeek from going into the second verse.

That left me free to jam my fingers into the control panel.

"Hurry, Noodle, I'm running out of words!"

I flipped every switch I could find. Finally I hit the right one—*sssssssss!* The robot ground to a stop, inches from Zeek. His control panel sizzled. His lights flashed. His gears wound down. Then nothing.

"You big . . . scrapheap!" I said.

Zeek hit the remote and the door opened. "Come on, buddy. We've got a job to do."

That's when the robot made his last move.

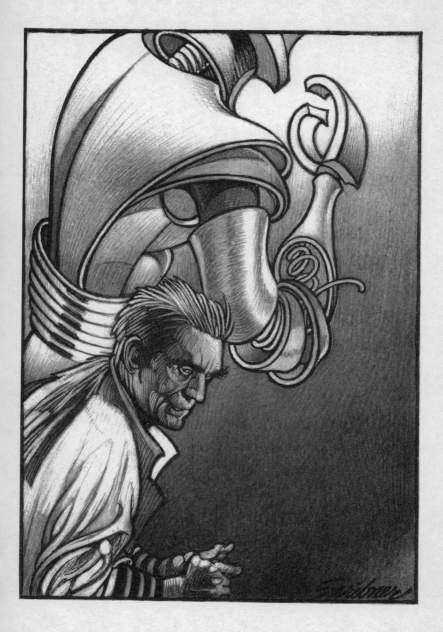

SEVEN

Primus twitched and I screamed.

"He's alive!"

In a flash the robot's middle arm shot up and punched a red button on the wall. Then he fell silent.

Suddenly, the floor started to rumble.

Weee—weee—weee! An alarm went off. Lights started flashing all over the laboratory.

"Self-destruct! The whole place is going to blow!" cried Zeek.

"Quick," I yelled. "The door is closing! We'd better hurry!"

We dived over the robot and leaped out the door an instant before it slammed shut. We hit the floor running.

We found ourselves in a narrow passage lined with huge electric generators. They were going crazy. Sparks were flying everywhere. The whole corridor was flashing red and blue.

At the end of the passage I could see a sign. It read: LAUNCH ROOM—KEEP OUT!

"That's it!" I cried. "We've got to stop Morbius!"

Zeek pulled the remote from his pocket and zapped the door. It slid open and we dashed in just as a fireball came shooting up the corridor. The door closed behind us.

We looked around.

"Holy cow!" I gasped. Zeek's mouth fell open. I guess he agreed with me.

It was the rocket command room. Rows and rows of computer stations circled a big screen.

At the far end of the room was a long ramp.

"Oh, no!" Zeek nudged me. "He's *serious*!"

Yeah, it was the little purple rocket, all right.

But it was different. On the back of it was a silver engine the size of one of those tanks they use to blow up helium balloons.

"The Morbius Booster," I gasped. "It looks pretty powerful."

And that wasn't the only difference. Strapped under each green fin was a stubby black can.

"You know what those are, don't you, Zeek?"

"Don't tell me."

"Bombs."

"I knew it!" Zeek whispered. "He's crazy."

"That's the word," I said.

Then something moved.

"No, boys, the word is *genius*. That's what they'll call me when they see what I can do!"

It was Morbius. He stepped out from the shadows. He pointed a funny-looking weapon at us.

"But it's nothing to the thrill I'll get when I drop those bombs!"

"No way, Ray!" I shouted. I grabbed Zeek's Fizz Blaster 2000 and aimed it at Morbius. "Zeekie, jump in!"

Zeek looked at me. "Jump in? Where?"

"The rocket. I've got a plan!"

Zeek started to run.

"Little troublemakers!" Morbius cried. "This rocket is programmed to drop those bombs. Nothing you can do will stop that! I can zap you into dust if I want to."

He hit the trigger on his gun and a thin green ray shot out. It blew a big hole in the floor near my feet.

I pumped the Blaster. "Zeek, the robot trick!"

"You mean sing?"

"No, the trick with the knees!"

Zeek punched his thumb in the air and started to run. Morbius followed him with his zapper, but Zeekie, the football star, dodged every shot.

Then I let go with a spray that saturated Morbius.

He whirled back around to shoot at me, but Zeek hit his knees from behind and he went stumbling forward.

"Now!" I shouted. "Into the rocket!"

I tossed the incredible Fizz Blaster 2000 to Zeek and we bounded across the room and into the rocket. I flipped all of the switches and punched all of the buttons and pulled all of the levers I could find.

Suddenly the door burst open.

"Oh-oh. He's back!" It was the robot. And he was glowing red-hot.

"Primus!" shouted Morbius. "Stop them!"

Kkk-thunk. Kkk-thunk.

Primus started up the ramp.

But Zeek blasted the floor in front of him and the robot slid back into Morbius, just as another shot left the ray gun.

Zap! The green beam went wild.

"All right! The Zeek Man scores!"

Suddenly, I hit the right button and the booster fired up. Morbius started screaming.

"You can't do that! IT'S MY ROCKET!"

The little purple rocket jolted up the ramp.

Green rays were exploding all around us.

"Step on it, Noodle!"

I closed the cockpit cover.

I hit the stick.

And the rocket blasted through the hatch and out into the air.

John Scribner © 93

EIGHT

We shot up instantly.

"Tell me what you see!" Zeek yelled. "I can't look!"

"Playground . . ." I said.

"Okay."

"School . . ."

"Yeah."

"Mayville . . ."

"Oh?"

"Clouds . . ."

"Noodle, don't say it!"

"Moon . . ."

"Noodle, stop!" He opened his eyes.

The speed was incredible. My stomach was somewhere on the ground. My face was stretching back into the seat. I turned to look at Zeek. He looked real funny.

We were shooting through the atmosphere like an arrow. Mayville was already far below us.

"Well," I said, "at least this time the rocket is going straight."

Zeek turned to face me. He had a look. "It's going straight, all right. *Straight up!* Can't you stop this thing?"

For once I didn't have a plan. I had tried everything. The switches. The buttons. The levers. The sticks. Nothing seemed to work now.

"Zeek, we must be on automatic pilot. Morbius is really controlling the rocket. I can't change course."

"So what do we do? Wait for it to crash?"

I didn't like to think about that. The booster was blasting away loudly behind us.

"Um . . . Zeek? I don't like those noises."

"Well, of course you don't. We're flying to outer space in a toy. *Noodle, this is a toy!*"

"At least we'll be famous," I said, trying to make him feel better. "Two kids who blasted off in a toy and—"

"And were lost in space forever!" said Zeek. He slammed his fist down on the control board.

When he did that, a hidden panel slid down in front of him.

"A radio! Noodle, it's a radio. We're saved! We can phone home, just like E.T. They'll send up the Space Shuttle and save us!"

I picked up the microphone, flipped a switch next to it, and started speaking. "Hello. Hello. This is Noodle Newton. I'm with my friend Zeek Pilinsky and we're in this rocket and we need help to get back to Earth. Hello, Air Force. Marines. Army. Coast Guard. FBI. PTA. Mom. Dad. Anybody. Come in. Over!"

We waited. Suddenly, the radio crackled in response. And a familiar sound came from the speaker.

"*Aaa-choo!* Hello, space cadets. Are you enjoying yourselves?"

"It's that rat, Morbius," Zeek said.

"I heard that," the voice snarled. "Don't worry. You'll come back soon. The next phase of your flight will begin shortly. Good-bye, boys."

Then Morbius let out one of his creepy laughs and the radio went dead.

"Oh, terrific," Zeek said. "He laughs, and we're going to die."

Zeek looked pretty bad. He does this every once in a while when things look hopeless.

I looked over the side and saw the great huge mass of nothing all around us. Just blue. And here we were, the two of us in this toy, with blue space all around us. Maybe Zeek was right. But I tried to cheer him up.

"Look," I said. "Don't worry. We're probably being picked up on somebody's radar screen right now. It won't be long before—"

"Before they shoot us down? That's what they do to things they see on radar screens, you know."

Maybe he was right. Maybe we really were in trouble this time. It did look pretty bad. Zeek and me all alone in space. Earth getting smaller and smaller. I started to feel scared.

Then I turned and saw that Danger Guy patch on Zeek's shoulder.

And then I saw Zeek.

For some reason he had started pushing all of the buttons on the panel at once.

"You know, Noodle, you're right," he said. "We can't give up. If a computer is running this rocket, let's jam the computer. We can do it. I know we can!" Then he smiled at me and jabbed his thumb in the air.

I did, too. Yeah, what a team!

That's when Zeek noticed a little digital clock on one of the side panels.

He looked at his watch.

"Stupid clock," he said. "It says five o'clock. It's not five o'clock. Look, now it's going backward. Four-fifty-nine. Four-fifty-eight."

I took a look at the numbers. "Um . . . Zeek? That's not a clock. It's a timer."

Just then the radio crackled again. "*Aaa-choo!* Phase two of your flight has just begun."

I picked up the microphone. "Listen, Morbius. Tell me what we're programmed to blow up."

Morbius laughed his crazy laugh. "Why, Mayville School, of course!"

"You're not a genius, you're nutty," Zeek yelled. Then he switched off the radio.

Just then the timer hit 4 minutes, 30 seconds, and—*whooom!* Down we went, rocketing back into Earth's atmosphere at unbelievable speed.

Toward Mayville. Toward our school.

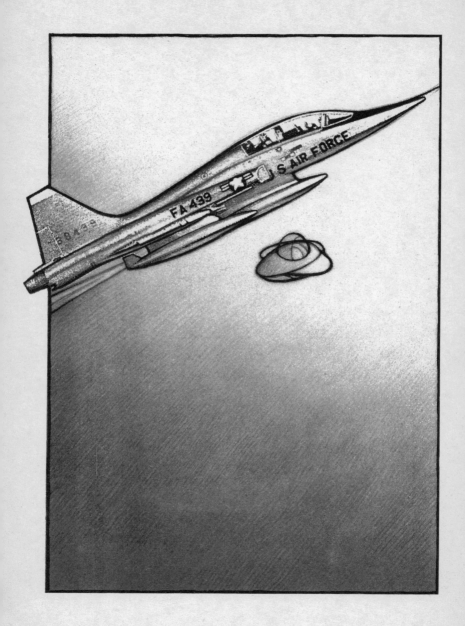

NINE

The force was unbelievable. The tip of the rocket was getting red from the heat. Our faces were doing funny things again.

In a flash we passed through the clouds.

Then there was a loud sound. But it wasn't us this time. I looked around. I nudged Zeek.

Behind us was a huge black jet. It was following close. Flames were coming out of its engines. There were attack rockets under each wing.

"I knew it," yelled Zeek. "They think we're the enemy and they're going to shoot us down!"

Then the pilot pulled alongside. I could see the American flag painted on a panel just under the cockpit. It made me want to cry.

The pilot held up his hand to me and gave me the okay sign with his fingers. Then he pointed behind him.

I looked there.

In the seat behind him were . . . my parents!

"They heard me calling them!"

I started to choke up, but Zeek said, "Look at the timer. It says two minutes!"

I held up two fingers to my parents to show that we only had two minutes left. They didn't get it. They each held up two fingers too.

"They think I'm giving them the peace sign."

"Yeah, the Rest-in-peace sign, you mean."

Then we dropped suddenly and the jet had to pull back.

We flashed down so fast I could hardly

breathe. We were headed straight for Mayville.

"Noodle, we've got to save our school. Do something! Your pocket! Look in your pocket!"

I dug in my pocket. I felt around. I didn't feel anything. All the junk from this morning was used up. I made a face.

"No! Don't tell me it's empty!" Zeek started pounding on the control panel. "We're all going to blow up!"

We were diving fast. I started feeling around again. There must be something. There must be!

Zeek was looking sick. He looked like he was ready to cry.

But then I started to smile. I felt something. I pulled out my hand. I held up . . . a paper clip!

"Hooray! I knew you had something. I knew you did!"

I got to work right away—the timer showed only thirty seconds left. I bent the paper clip into a J and jammed the long

end behind the timer. I figured that's
where the computer brains would be.

Fifteen seconds.

Twelve seconds.

Zeek held his breath.

Mayville School was dead ahead.

I wiggled the paper clip.

Ten seconds.

Five seconds.

I wiggled it some more.

Two seconds.

64

TEN

*C*lick!

The timer stopped. One second to spare. It was over.

I pulled up on the control stick and we leveled off just over the school roof.

"Yippee! The Noodle Man does it again! Incredible!" Zeek laughed and slapped me on the back.

Not a good thing to do.

Whooom! The rocket dipped and fell about twenty feet.

"Whoa, Zeek. We've still got the bombs on board! If we hit anything or crash-land, it's so long, Mayville. Better start looking around for somewhere safe to dump the bombs."

I turned the control stick.

"Hey, that's my house," Zeek mumbled.

"Yeah, but I don't think your mom wants bombs in her yard."

"That's my house," Zeek said again.

"Sure, terrific view. But listen, Zeek, we're running out of time here, okay?"

"No, that's my *house*!" Zeek repeated. He seemed really excited, so I decided to look.

That's when I got what he meant.

"Zeek, that's your *house*!"

It was his house, all right. And we were zooming straight for it.

Not only that. We were headed straight for the front door. And not only that. We were headed straight for the front door at the same time that Zeek's mom opened it and looked out.

What happened next went incredibly fast.

We shot in the front door, just as Zeek's

mom stepped out of the way to answer the phone, at the same time that Zeek's little sister dropped her doll on the floor and Zeek's dad, who was just opening the back door, bent down to pick it up.

We were through the room and out the back door in a flash.

No one would have seen us at all except that Zeek yelled out, "Hi Mom! Hi Dad! Hi Em!" at the top of his lungs when we went through, and everyone turned to see a blurry purple thing blast through the living room.

Once we were through, I pulled the stick back to lift us clear of the trees in the backyard. It worked. We shot high over the mall and over the woods on the far side.

"Whew! That was a close one, no?" I smiled at Zeek. Yeah, things were picking up.

"Over there," he said. He pointed to a shiny blue patch of water just north of the woods.

"Feather Lake!" I said.

"Sure, it's deserted this time of year. Perfect."

I twisted the control stick slightly until the lake was straight ahead. I was obviously getting pretty good at this.

When we were right over it, Zeek pulled the manual release. The two bombs dropped into the lake.

Wump! Wump! Two muffled explosions rippled the water. Then the lake went calm again. "Perfect," Zeek breathed.

Just then the radio came on. It was you-know-who.

"Why, you little brats! I'll show you. And this time no one will stop me!" Then the radio shut off.

I looked over at Zeek. He looked at me and started to smile a big, long smile. Yeah, it felt good to see that we were both thinking the same thing.

"Stop that nutball, Noodle!"

"Yeah, and his little robot, too!"

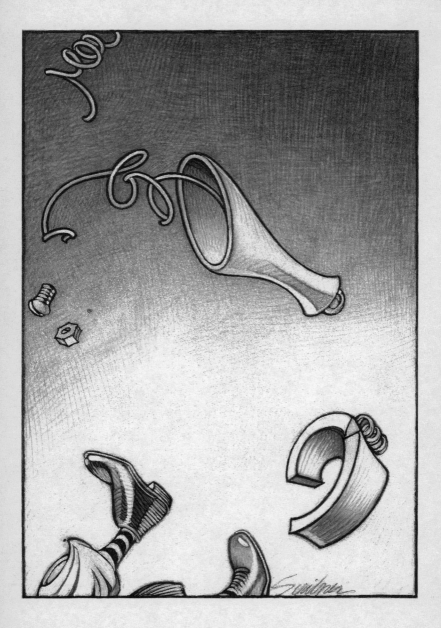

ELEVEN

I looped the rocket around and took off for Mayville center.

If Morbius had radioed from his laboratory, it wouldn't take him long to get to where I knew he was going. I had to try to cut him off.

Then I glanced at the fuel gauge. E for empty.

The booster suddenly sputtered. We started to drop over Main Street.

"Oh, please, just a few more minutes."

There was the carnival. The white lights. The rides. It seemed like a year since we'd been there. And it had been just that morning.

Then, just as we coasted over, Zeek spotted them. "Look, Noodle! It's Morbius. And Primus. They've stolen another rocket. And they've got more bombs!"

I could see them dead ahead. Morbius had attached a portable booster to one of the other rockets. He fired it up and pulled away from the ride in a blast of smoke.

"Zeek, we've got one chance to wreck their booster. Our fuel tanks are empty. My pockets are empty. How about your Blaster? Any ammo left?"

He shook the Blaster. Not good. But he started pumping, anyway.

I threw the control stick forward as hard as I could. We lunged toward them.

Primus was steering their rocket. Morbius turned when he saw us and fired his ray gun.

Zaaap! The green ray hit a bunch of balloons behind us. They exploded like fireworks.

I stayed on them. Zeek lowered the Blaster and took aim.

"Dogfight!" I yelled.

Fizz fizz fizz! The last jet stream shot from Zeek's gun like a bullet and hit Morbius's booster dead in the center.

BOOM! Their rocket flamed out and dropped. Primus lost control.

Zeek and I skidded to a stop near the curly french-fries stand. Morbius's rocket bounced against the hamburger grill and he and Primus flew out. Primus went really high.

Morbius flipped over a dozen times in midair before he came down.

Then I heard that familiar sound.

Ping!

Morbius's head hit the bell on the Test-Your-Strength game. He landed in a heap at the bottom.

The crowd cheered.

A few seconds later they handed me my prize—a Fizz Blaster 2000, just like Zeek's.

"Yeah, Zeek," I said. "I guess we've got the right stuff!"

That's when Primus finally landed. He

fell on the bandstand. And in the food tent. And by the pony rides. And in the parking lot.

Zeek turned to me. "He's kind of broken up about the whole thing!"

I had to laugh. "Yeah, I guess he just lost his head!"

Within seconds the army moved in and took Morbius away in a security truck. They came later with a dump truck for the big silver guy.

On our way home in an army jeep, Zeek and I got thoughtful.

"Poor Mr. Vazny," I said. "Maybe if he stops being so mad, he could make some neat stuff to help people."

"Cool. Like robots that bring you lunch." Then Zeek started to smile. "You know, Noodle?"

"What?" I said.

"This has been a pretty cool day."

I had to agree. "We almost didn't make it a couple times. And I was pretty scared up there. But yeah, I had fun."

"Maybe we could do it again some-time?"

We ate at my house that night.

Waffles, of course. I needed them after an adventure like that.

My mom and dad were still telling Zeek's parents about their trip in the jet. And Zeek's parents were still talking about the purple flash that went through their living room.

So it was tough trying to tell anybody about what had happened to Zeek and me. But that's okay. Sometimes you just have to let parents talk.

Later, Ms. Hernandez, the principal, came over. She wanted to thank us personally for saving the school. And that was just the beginning. The local TV crew came over, too.

The reporter asked us about what had happened, so we told her the whole story. Then Zeek filled his Blaster in the bathroom and took everybody outside to show off some fancy shooting.

Just as the reporter was packing up, she asked, "With all these adventures you've been having, what would you boys like to do when you grow up?"

"I don't know," I said. "Same kind of stuff."

I looked over at Zeek. He was nodding and smiling a big smile. He gave me the thumbs-up. "Well, Noodle," he said. "It's been a day. See you tomorrow."

I grinned and turned to go inside.

"Oh, Noodle?" he said. "Just one more thing."

I turned around.

That's when he got me. All down my shirt. A blast to end all blasts!

I reached for my own Blaster.

Yeah, that's Zeek and me.

Danger Guys forever.

**Don't miss the next
dangerous adventure:**

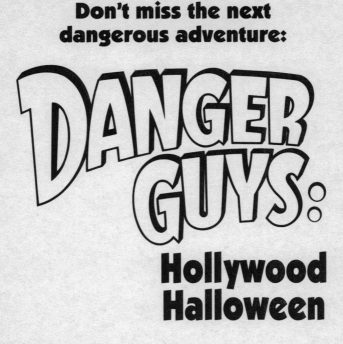

Hollywood
Halloween

 Noodle and Zeek are making a Hollywood
movie of their own.

 But lightning strikes on a trip to Paragon
Studios, and the Danger Guys are thrust into
a movie of someone else's making.

 A cast of thousands descends—a dinosaur
in Gorgatron Park; a killer cyborg from the
future; a moaning mummy and an army of
sword-wielding skeletons.

 The Danger Guys must find a way to bring
this movie to a close . . . and to save
their lives.